Stop That Eyeball!

Read other

SPENCER'S
adventures

#1 Stop That Eyeball!

• • • • • • coming soon • • • • • •

#2 Garbage Snooper Surprise

SPENCER'S adventures

Stop That Eyeball!

by

Gary Hogg

Illustrated by Chuck Slack

A
LITTLE APPLE
PAPERBACK

SCHOLASTIC INC.
New York   Toronto   London   Auckland   Sydney

ISBN 0–590–93935–1

Text copyright © 1995 by Gary Hogg.
Illustrations copyright © 1996 by Scholastic Inc.
All rights reserved. Published by Scholastic Inc.
LITTLE APPLE PAPERBACKS and the LITTLE APPLE PAPERBACKS logo are trademarks of Scholastic Inc.

12 11 10 9 8 7 6 5 4 3 2   6 7 8 9/9 0 1/0

Printed in the U.S.A.   40

First Scholastic printing, October 1996

For my son Jonah,
a boy who makes me laugh every day.

CONTENTS

· · · · · · · · · · · · · · · · ·

Chapter One

Macaroni Masterpiece

"It's finished," shouted Spencer as he glued the last noodle into place. "My macaroni dinosaur is finally done."

Building a dinosaur completely out of macaroni had been tough. Spencer had spent two weeks and used over ten bags of macaroni to complete his masterpiece. But it would all be worth it if he could win the grand prize at

Crestview Elementary School's Annual Art Show and Contest.

Spencer stood back, marveling at the beauty of his creation. "This is one awesome dinosaur," said Spencer. He ran out to get his family.

Proudly, Spencer led his mom, dad, and sister into the bedroom. "What do you think?" he asked. "Do you think I'll win the contest? Do you? Do you? Do you?"

Mr. Burton studied the dinosaur thoughtfully. "Son, you certainly have a way with macaroni. I think you have a winner."

"His name is Victor and you haven't even seen the best part yet," said Spencer. He grabbed hold of the dinosaur's tail and began pumping it up and down.

"Look, how cute," said Mrs. Burton. "It can wag its tail, just like a dog."

"Hey, it's a dogosaurus," laughed Spencer's sister, Amber.

"It is not," said Spencer, pumping even faster. Suddenly a bright purple liquid squirted out of Victor's mouth and nose.

"Oh, gross!" screamed his sister. "That thing just slobbered all over Dad."

"Spencer," said his mother sharply. "Your dinothing has just ruined your father's good white shirt."

Spencer laughed. "Don't worry, Mom, it's just grape juice." He gave the tail three more good pumps, and the dinosaur sprayed juice into Spencer's mouth.

"Grape juice?" moaned his mother.

"Yeah, it's supposed to be poison. Victor sprays it on his victims. It paralyzes them so he can move in for the kill."

"Hey," said Spencer's dad, "I can't

move. The poison is taking effect. Save me before the dinodog attacks."

Everyone began to laugh, and Spencer sprayed more grape juice into his mouth.

"When the judge gets a load of Victor," said Spencer, "he'll make me the winner for sure."

"Oh, yeah," laughed Amber. "When the judge gets a face full of dinosaur slobber, I'm sure he'll be very impressed."

"You're just jealous because Victor is a better project than that dumb painting of yours," said Spencer.

"It is not a dumb painting," she said. "It's the 'Mona Pizza.' It has style. Mom even said so."

"A painting of a pizza with pepperoni making the face of an old lady is not my idea of style," said Spencer.

"It's better than a slobbering macaroni dinodog."

"Spencer and Amber, that is enough," said Mr. Burton. "You both have very nice projects. I'm sure you will both do well at the art contest."

"Spencer, I suggest you put your dinosaur in a safe place," said his mother. "The art show isn't until tomorrow night and we don't want The Terminator to get hold of it."

The Terminator was Spencer's two-year-old brother. His name was Jake and he was a one-boy wrecking crew. Wherever Jake toddled, terror soon followed.

"Don't worry, Mom," said Spencer. "I'm going to keep Victor in my bedroom with the door closed tight. He'll be as safe as money in the bank."

Chapter Two

Sweet Dreams

It took Spencer a long time to fall asleep that night. He couldn't stop thinking about how well Victor had turned out. When he finally did drift off, Spencer dreamed about the art show.

In his dream, the school gymnasium was full of excited people. They were all dressed in church clothes and drinking punch from tall, fancy glasses.

Several TV cameras and a group of reporters were gathered around Spencer and his dinosaur. They were all talking at once.

"Please," said Spencer. "I can only answer one question at a time."

A beautiful lady reporter raised her hand. "How did you make your dinosaur so lifelike?"

"It's all in the noodle selection," answered Spencer. "You can't just throw macaroni together. Each noodle was carefully chosen."

"In the future, do you plan to work with any other food groups?" asked a hungry-looking reporter.

"Yes, but I'm keeping it a secret. All I can tell you is that it involves french fries and a lot of maple syrup."

Suddenly the principal's voice came over the loudspeaker. "Ladies and gentlemen, thank you for coming. As

8

you can see, Crestview Elementary is blessed with many talented artists. And now, to choose our grand champion, let me introduce professional artist and judge, Mack A. Roni."

The judge went right to work. He whirled down the rows, quickly judging each project.

He told Whitney Jones that the characters in her painting were stiff and boring.

"But I'm only in first grade," she said.

"Well, grow up," he snapped back.

The judge looked at Josh Porter's statue of a gopher and said, "Don't quit your day job."

"I don't have a day job," said Josh.

"I can see why," replied the judge.

He took one look at Amber's "Mona Pizza" and started to gag. "Quick, remove this from the building before I throw up."

When the judge came to Spencer, he stopped. "And what do we have here?" he asked.

"Your Honor, may I present Victor," said Spencer proudly.

"My, my," said Mr. Roni. "I do like this. It seems to speak to me."

"There's more," said Spencer, pumping the tail. As the grape juice sprayed from Victor's nose, the judge began applauding.

"Bravo, bravo!" shouted the judge. "Quick, get me a glass."

He filled the glass from Victor's nose and raised it high so everyone could see. "A toast to Spencer and his wonderful dinosaur!"

Everyone cheered and chanted, "Spencer, Spencer, Spencer." The chanting became louder. It shook the building. It was shaking Spencer.

Spencer opened his eyes. It wasn't

the cheering that was shaking him, it was his mother.

"Spencer, for the last time, wake up," she said. "You are going to be late for school."

"Oh, no!" gasped Spencer as he looked at his clock. He had overslept.

Spencer jumped out of bed and raced to the kitchen. He wolfed down his breakfast. Dashing back to his room, he threw on his school clothes, grabbed his backpack, and hurried off to school.

In the rush, he forgot to close his bedroom door.

Chapter Three

Dinosaur Picnic

The Terminator was having his usual day. He had broken a lamp and a vase and chewed a hole in the drapes.

His mother was busy cleaning up his latest mess when Jake started down the hall. He spotted Spencer's open door and toddled in.

The Terminator wandered around the room looking for something to break.

Spencer always tried to keep his

room Jake-proof. Everything he owned, including Victor, was perched safely on shelves well out of Jake's reach. Victor seemed to be resting comfortably.

When Jake spotted the dinosaur, he let out a squeal. Victor just sat there quietly. He had no idea that he was about to become extinct. Someday it will be proven that a tribe of little Jakes brought an end to all dinosaurs.

The Terminator stretched as high as he could, but the dinosaur was out of reach. He pulled the chair out from Spencer's desk and slid it under the shelf.

Standing on the chair, reaching as high as he could, Jake still couldn't touch the dinosaur. He rocked back, banging the chair into the wall. The wall shook and Victor moved closer to the edge of the shelf.

Jake rocked and crashed, rocked and

crashed until the dinosaur was teetering on the edge of the shelf. One final crash of the chair sent Victor flying.

The dinosaur landed on a blanket next to the chair. Jake hopped down, bent over, and looked Victor in the eye. For the first time in his short life, Victor knew fear.

The battle was a fierce one. It was boy against macaroni. The Terminator made the first move. He grabbed Victor by his long spaghetti neck and shook him.

Victor fought back, spilling grape juice all over Jake. Jake tasted the juice and began sucking on Victor's nose.

"Juice, juice," cried Jake. He couldn't have been happier.

When Victor finally ran out of juice, the fight turned ugly. Jake threw Victor high into the air. "Doggie fly," he said.

Victor flew across the room and smashed into the wall, breaking off one leg. "Doggie have owie," said Jake.

He picked up the leg and made an exciting discovery. Victor was made out of his favorite lunch — macaroni.

"Roni," said Jake excitedly. "Jake like ronis."

It didn't take Jake long to break Victor into nice, bite-sized pieces. The Terminator sat down and had a delicious dinosaur picnic.

Chapter Four

Mom, Jake Ate My Dinosaur

When Spencer came home from school, he headed straight for his bedroom. Coming down the hall, he saw his open bedroom door. His heart began to pound.

"Oh, I hope it's not The Terminator," he said. "Please, don't let it be The Terminator."

But the moment Spencer entered his

bedroom, he knew that his worst nightmare had come true. Sitting in the middle of the floor was Jake. He had Victor's tail clenched between his teeth and a leg in each hand.

"MOM, Jake ate my dinosaur!" screamed Spencer.

When Jake looked at Spencer and saw smoke coming out of his ears, he started to shake. Even a Terminator knows when to run and hide.

Crawling quickly, Jake headed under the bed. Spencer caught him by the leg and dragged him out, squirming and squealing like a pig. Jake spun around and bit Spencer on the arm.

Spencer let out a yell and Jake headed for the door. "Oh no you don't!" screamed Spencer, leaping on his brother. "Now I've got you."

Before Jake could bite him again,

Spencer put the toddler in a headlock.

"You little creep," said Spencer, pounding on the top of Jake's head. "How would you like it if I ate your tricycle?"

"Spencer, you let go of your little brother this instant!" ordered Mrs. Burton as she entered the room.

"But Mom, he ate my art project!"

"I can see that. But you shouldn't have left your bedroom door open. Now turn him loose or you can forget about going to the art show tonight."

Spencer loosened his grip and The Terminator scrambled for the safety of the living room.

"Can't we sell him to a wrecking yard or something?"

"Don't be silly. You love your brother and you know it."

"I don't love him eating my stuff."

"Spencer, there is still some time be-

fore the art show begins. Why don't you glue your dinosaur back together?"

"I can't glue my dinosaur back together. All of the best parts are in Jake's stomach."

"Well, maybe you could make something a little quicker and easier than a dinosaur. How about a lizard or a pickle? I think a little green macaroni pickle might be just the ticket."

"MOTHER! A real live artist is judging the contest. I don't think he would be impressed with a stupid-looking macaroni pickle."

"Suit yourself, but I don't see how you expect to win the contest if you don't even enter."

Suddenly a loud banging noise came from the living room. "It sounds like your brother is on another crash course. I'd better go."

Spencer sat down on the floor and stared at the carpet. He wanted to enter this contest more than anything in the whole world. He was so depressed.

Chapter Five

That's the Way the Ball Bounces

Spencer picked a piece of macaroni up off the floor and put it in his mouth. Chewing on the noodle, he began to think.

His mother was right. Victor was a goner. If he was going to have an entry for the art show, he would have to get to work quick.

"I can't paint a picture. Amber will say I copied her," thought Spencer. "Of course, any picture that I'd paint would be a thousand times better than her stupid picture.

"I could carve something out of wood." He glanced at his hands. "No, I might slip and carve one of my fingers instead. The sight of blood and bandages might throw the judge off a little bit.

"I could mold something out of clay," he thought. Then Spencer remembered the time he molded a snake out of clay.

The little brown snake was very realistic-looking. It had a forked tongue and beady little eyes. Spencer had coiled the snake and set it on the living room floor. He wanted to see if it would scare anyone.

It scared someone, all right. When Spencer's mom saw it, she thought that Buck, the family dog, had had an accident.

She chased him out of the house with a broom. When she came back, Jake had the snake in his mouth. His mother dropped the broom and cried, "Oh my, oh my," a couple of times and fainted.

Clay was out for sure. Spencer didn't need his mother fainting in front of everyone at the school.

He could make a fantastic moose out of pinecones. On second thought, it would take several hours to make a decent pinecone moose. And Spencer didn't have that kind of time.

Spencer looked hopefully around his room. In the corner, some dirty socks and underwear were piled on top of his basketball.

"I wish Jake would have eaten those socks instead of my dinosaur," said Spencer. "It would serve him right to have dirty sock breath."

He grabbed the socks and underwear and threw them in his closet. Spencer picked up the basketball and began bouncing it.

Hey, I could create macaroni underwear, he thought. I'd just glue macaroni all over a pair of undershorts. If I didn't win the art contest, at least I would end up with something useful. I could wear them when I go camping. That way, if I get lost, I won't starve. I'll just cook up an underwear casserole.

Spencer threw the basketball into the closet. It hit the edge of the shelf and came shooting back at him. The ball smacked Spencer right in the face.

"Ouch!" he yelled. "You stupid ball, watch where you're going."

Behind him, Spencer heard his least favorite sound. Amber was standing in the doorway, laughing at him.

"You dummy," she said, giggling. "It can't watch where it's going. It's a basketball, not an eyeball."

"I know that," said Spencer, firing the ball at his sister.

Amber slammed the door just in time. The basketball hit the door and bounced back at Spencer.

"It would be awesome if it really were a gaint eyeball," Spencer said to himself. "When I played basketball, I'd make every shot because the ball could see where it was going."

Spencer picked up the basketball and examined it. "I'll bet dinosaurs had eyeballs about this big.

"Hey, wait a minute. With a little bit of time and a lot of macaroni, I could turn this ball into a terrific-looking dinosaur eyeball. I'll bet that would win the art contest for sure."

Spencer was back in the art business.

Chapter Six

A Very Sticky Situation

Spencer went right to work. He had less than an hour to create a new masterpiece.

"I need macaroni," he said, "lots and lots of macaroni."

Spencer ran to the kitchen and rounded up every last noodle in the house. He loaded a grocery bag with elbow macaroni and macaroni spirals, wheels, and shells.

"I hope Mom wasn't planning on making that tuna and noodles junk tonight," thought Spencer.

He took the bag back to his room and threw it on the bed. "Now, I need a great big bucket of super sticky glue."

Spencer knew right where to go. His dad was always using glue to fix the things Jake broke. "There should be a ton of glue in Dad's workshop," he said.

"Glue, glue, where are you?" said Spencer as he entered the workshop. He saw jugs of glue, jars of glue, tubes of glue, and glue sticks.

Then Spencer spotted exactly what he was looking for. It was the big bucket of homemade glue that Uncle Tony had whipped up especially for Spencer's dad. Uncle Tony called it his Super Dooper Stick-To-It-Glue.

"This stuff could stick a tornado to the ground," bragged Uncle Tony. "The only drawback is that it gives off a slight odor."

Spencer remembered the first time his mom got a whiff of that slight odor. She had turned green and made a dash for the bathroom.

Spencer dragged the bucket back to his room. He set the basketball on his bed and announced, "Ladies and gentlemen, right before your eyes, I will turn this ordinary basketball into an amazing, life-size dinosaur eyeball."

Spencer pried the lid off the glue bucket. "Whew, this stuff really *is* a stinkeroo," he said as he stuck his hands deep into the goo. He pulled out two handfuls and smeared the glue on the basketball.

Spencer worked as fast as he could.

Glue slopped everywhere. For every glob of glue he got on the basketball, Spencer got two globs on himself. By the time the basketball was covered with glue, Spencer was covered with glue, too.

"And now for some macaroni," said Spencer picking up a handful of noodles. His hands were so sticky he couldn't get the macaroni off of them and onto the basketball. He tried slapping. He tried throwing. He tried whipping.

"Hmmm," said Spencer, "I need a noodle shooter." Bending over, he poked his head into the bag of macaroni. Filling both cheeks, he began shooting noodles at the basketball out of his mouth.

Ratta-tat-tat, noodle after noodle splatted on the ball. Spencer reloaded and fired another round. Soon the basketball was covered with macaroni.

"All it needs now is a little color,"
said Spencer. He took a quick glance at
the clock and went to find some paint.

Chapter Seven

The Human Magnet

Spencer slowly opened his door and peeked out. He thought it might be better if his mom didn't see him looking like a walking glob of glue.

He looked both ways and called softly, "Mom?" No answer. Spencer stepped out into the hall.

Remembering that he had seen a can of paint in the cupboard above the refrigerator, Spencer headed for the kitchen. He crept down the hall and peeked around the corner.

"Mom, are you in there?" he called softly into the kitchen. There was no answer. "Great," he whispered, and started across the kitchen floor.

Walking across the floor was like walking in mud. With each step, his glue-covered shoes stuck to the white tile floor.

"Spencer, are you in the kitchen?" his mother called from the next room.

Spencer froze in his sticky tracks.

"Yes, Mom," he replied reluctantly.

"What are you tearing? It sounds like you are ripping something."

"I'm just working on my new art project."

"Oh good, I'll come right in and help you."

"NO!" yelled Spencer, trying not to panic. "I don't want you to see me — I mean, *it* — until I'm finished. Please, stay in the living room."

"All right, son, don't come unglued. I'll leave you alone. Let me know as soon as you're finished. I'm dying to see this new masterpiece. I'm proud of you for sticking to it."

Spencer slid a chair over to the counter and jumped up on it. He put his belly against the silverware drawer and rolled onto the top of the counter.

Spencer was a human magnet. When he stood up, two dirty spoons, a set of car keys, and Amber's retainer were all clinging to his glue-covered clothes.

Opening the cupboard above the refrigerator, Spencer started shoving things around. There wasn't any paint, but he found some wonderful things.

Carefully hidden behind a bag of marshmallows was Spencer's favorite squirt gun. It had disappeared the day he loaded it with pickle juice and squirted Aunt Marge.

Next to the gun was a cup full of fake worms. Spencer hadn't seen those since the time he slipped them in Grandma's bowl of chicken noodle soup.

"I'll be back for you guys later," said Spencer as he jumped down and headed for the garage.

On his way to the garage, Spencer stopped by the laundry room. Last week, The Terminator had created some artwork of his own on the wall next to the clothes dryer. After his dad re-painted the wall, Spencer thought, he might have left the can of paint on the shelf above the washing machine.

Spencer tried a running leap onto the washer, but missed. He fell backwards into a pile of laundry. When he stood up, two orange socks and a pair of his dad's undershorts were plastered to the back of his shirt.

Spencer jumped again and made it to the top of the washer. He inspected the shelf and found the markers that Jake had used to draw on the wall, but there was no paint. Spencer hopped down and headed for the garage.

In the garage, Spencer hit the jackpot. On the shelf with the cleaning supplies he found two cans of paint.

"Great," said Spencer, looking them over. "I have black and red, now all I need is some white."

Spencer looked around the garage. On the shelf above the garden tools, he spotted a large can of white paint.

He stacked the can of red paint on the black and stepped up on top of them.

Spencer waited until the cans quit rocking and then announced, "Ladies

and gentlemen, The Magnificent Spencer will bravely snatch the mystical can from the Shelf of Death."

Just as his sticky fingers got a grip on the big can of paint, Jake came toddling into the garage. Spencer gasped.

"Get out of here! Don't come near me, you little brat."

Jake made a beeline for Spencer balancing on the cans of paint.

"Oh no!" yelled Spencer, losing his grip and tumbling to the floor.

The Magnificent Spencer found himself sitting under a waterfall of white paint. The paint covered his head, flowed over his face, and splattered on the floor.

The Terminator stood staring at Spencer, and then he started to laugh. "Spencer fall down, go boom. Do it more, Spencer. Do it more."

As Spencer got to his feet, Jake

wisely left the garage. He didn't want to end up in another headlock.

Spencer took one look at the mess and made a quick decision. He put it on the list of messes he would take care of later. Right now, he had to finish his art project. There was not a minute to lose.

Chapter Eight

Mr. Boobles, Meet Mr. Paint

Holding a can of paint in each hand and one under his arm, Spencer headed into the backyard. He stepped through the flower beds next to the house until he came to the window of his room.

Spencer tossed the cans of paint through the open window. With one foot on the water spigot, he pushed himself onto the windowsill. A couple of wiggles later, he fell off of the sill onto the floor of his bedroom.

As Spencer pushed himself up off the floor, he came eye to eye with his art project. "Awesome," said Spencer. "With a little paint, you'll be a winner for sure."

Spencer hunted down his Swiss Army knife and used it to pry the lids off the paint cans.

"Now I need something to paint with," he said, looking around the room. There, lying helplessly on the floor, was Jake's favorite stuffed bunny, Mr. Boobles. Spencer grabbed the bunny by the ears.

"Mr. Boobles, meet Mr. Paint," said Spencer as he dunked Mr. Boobles' head in the black paint. Rubbing the dripping wet head on the eyeball,

Spencer created a big black pupil.

Suddenly, there was a loud knock on the door.

"Stay out!" screamed Spencer.

"Spencer, it's Mom. Have you seen my car keys?"

"Last time I saw them, they were on the kitchen counter."

"Well, they have mysteriously disappeared."

"Maybe Jake ate them," joked Spencer.

"I guess we'll have to take your father's car. Are you ready to go? We have to leave right now or we might be late."

Spencer knew that his dad would not let him get in the car without taking a bath first. And he didn't have that kind of time.

"I have a couple of things left to do.

Go without me and I'll come over as soon as I'm done."

"All right, but hurry as fast as you can. You don't want to miss the judging," said his mother as she left.

Spencer dabbed what was left of the white paint onto the eyeball. Then he dipped Mr. Boobles' long foot in the red paint and added some squiggly lines.

"You look so real, it's almost spooky," said Spencer, picking up the wet eyeball and dashing out of the house.

Chapter Nine

Son of Big Foot

Spencer jumped off the back porch and cut through the driveway. He eyed the basketball hoop and pretended to shoot the dinosaur eyeball at the basket.

"Swish," he hollered. "Nothing but net. This eyeball just can't miss."

Spencer was so excited about his new creation, he felt as if he were running on air as he headed for the school. Even his sticky clothes and shoes couldn't slow him down.

"Here comes the Eyeball Express," shouted Spencer as he zoomed down the street. To save time, he decided to take his secret shortcut.

The shortcut went through three of the most dangerous yards in the neighborhood.

Mrs. Martin had a St. Bernard. Mr. Peterson had two German shepherds. And Mrs. Hiskey had the most dangerous creature of all. She had Mr. Hiskey.

Spencer ducked under the Martins' big pine tree and streaked through the yard. With a deep-sounding *woof*, the St. Bernard started after him. In no time at all, the mutt's slimy jaws were hot on Spencer's heels.

Spencer began high-stepping to avoid the dog's sharp teeth. With one final *woof,* the big dog hit the end of his chain and jerked to a stop.

"One down, two to go," gasped Spencer.

He stuffed the eyeball up the front of his shirt. Spencer would need both hands free to get past the Petersons' yard.

He jumped up onto the top rail of the Petersons' fence. With arms outstretched for balance, Spencer started walking along the top of the fence.

The German shepherds were growling and pacing back and forth under Spencer. It was fifty feet of torture. One small slip and he would be dog chow.

When he reached the other side, Spencer turned and barked wildly at the dogs. This always made them go nuts.

Spencer pulled the eyeball out of his shirt and dropped down off the fence. He landed right next to Mr. Hiskey's KEEP OUT sign.

Mr. Hiskey was just a little different. He not only believed in aliens, he was sure they had his address and phone number.

Spencer took a deep breath and started his dash across the yard. He was moving so fast, he didn't see the rake lying in the grass.

When Spencer's foot hit the rake, he went flying through the air. Luckily, he landed in a nice, soft pile of leaves.

The force of the fall knocked the eyeball loose. A couple of good bounces on the grass sent it shooting out of the yard. The dinosaur eyeball headed down the sidewalk, rolling at a high rate of speed.

Spencer got up as fast as he could.

He was dizzy from the crash and stumbled around in a circle.

At that moment, Mr. Hiskey happened to glance out his front window. He took one look at Spencer all covered with leaves, staggering around his yard, and yelled for his wife.

"See, Vera, I told you. I knew there was a Bigfoot living in the area."

"Horace," said Mrs. Hiskey, having a look for herself, "I don't know what that is, but it is definitely not Bigfoot. It's only four feet tall, for crying out loud."

"Well then," said Mr. Hiskey excitedly, "it's a baby Bigfoot. It's Little Foot, son of Bigfoot. Now, call the police before he gets away. Then bring me my camera. I have to get a picture of this strange, hideous creature."

Spencer regained his senses just in time to see the eyeball rolling down the sidewalk past a group of little girls. "Stop that eyeball!" bellowed Spencer.

At that instant, Mr. Hiskey came out of the house yelling, "Run for your life! It's Son of Bigfoot. Run for your life!"

The girls started screaming and ran away as fast as they could.

Spencer had no trouble outrunning old Mr. Hiskey. He had a harder time running down the eyeball. He caught up with it just before it crashed into the wall of the school.

"Whew," sighed Spencer as he picked up the eyeball. "I thought you were gone for good." He wiped as much dirt off as he could and dashed through the open door into the gymnasium.

Chapter Ten

Here Comes the Judge

As Spencer entered the gym, every head turned and every eye stared right at him.

He was covered with leaves and white paint. Two dirty spoons, his mom's car keys, Amber's retainer, and a pair of orange socks were sticking to his clothes like ornaments on a Christmas tree. To top it all off, a pair of his dad's undershorts was displayed for all to see.

Spencer took the eyeball and began walking to the end of the row. As he walked along, he noticed several macaroni dinosaurs. I sure hope this judge likes eyeballs, thought Spencer.

He walked past Amber, standing next to her "Mona Pizza." Her face was redder than the pepperoni in her painting.

Amber hissed something as Spencer walked past. He couldn't quite make it out. It was either, "You did it. I wish you luck," or "You idiot, I hate your guts."

Spencer walked to the end of the row and set the eyeball on the table.

He peered up into the bleachers, trying to locate his parents. It took him a minute to find them. His dad was slouched down, wiping his forehead with a handkerchief. His mother had her head shoved almost completely into her purse.

They must not have seen me yet, thought Spencer.

The judge was a funny-looking guy, nothing like the judge in Spencer's dream. He was very short and had a pointy little beard. He wore white tennis shoes and a striped turtleneck shirt.

He walked along the rows, slowly judging the art projects. As he studied the entries, he would say something encouraging to each student.

Spencer wished the judge would hurry up. He was nervous and beginning to sweat. The sweat, mixing with the paint and glue, was making Spencer feel extremely itchy.

Suddenly, like a crazed commando, Mr. Hiskey burst through the door of the gymnasium. Bug-eyed and breathing hard, he was accompanied by his wife and two policemen.

When Spencer spotted Mr. Hiskey, he ducked down and crawled under the table. He didn't think it would be a good idea to be seen right now by someone who thought he was some sort of hairy monster.

Everyone in the gymnasium stared at Mr. Hiskey as he tried to explain to the principal that a baby Bigfoot was hiding in the school.

"I assure you, sir," said Mr. Warner, "there is no Bigfoot in this school."

"But he came running through my yard not five minutes ago. I'm sure I saw him duck in here," blurted Mr. Hiskey.

"Now, Mr. Hiskey, if a Bigfoot had indeed entered this school, don't you think someone would have noticed?"

Mr. Hiskey took a big whiff of air.

"What about *that?*" he said. "Can't you smell that foul odor? That is the horrible stink of a baby Bigfoot."

"What you refer to as a foul odor is the lingering aroma of the fish sticks that were served at lunch," answered Mr. Warner sternly.

"Come on, Mr. Hiskey," said one of the officers. "I think these people are safe now. Let us take you back to your house. On the way you can tell us more about this evil creature."

When Mr. Hiskey left, Spencer came out from under the table. He looked up into the crowd. This time his mother and father were both glaring at him. He gave a little wave, but they didn't wave back.

Finally, the moment he had dreamed about was here. The judge was standing in front of Spencer and his dinosaur eyeball. Spencer stood up straight and turned the eyeball so that it was looking right at the judge.

"Very interesting," said the judge. But he wasn't looking at the eyeball. He was looking at Spencer.

He walked around Spencer three times. He looked at the car keys and said, "Creative."

He looked at Mr. Burton's under-shorts and said, "Original."

He looked at the paint and the leaves and the orange socks and exclaimed, "I love it!"

"Ladies and gentlemen, may I have your attention. This young man has created a modern masterpiece. I can tell you right now, he is the winner. He is the grand champion of the art contest."

Spencer was so happy, he started jumping up and down. Amber walked over and jerked her retainer off Spen-

cer's shirt. "Who gave you permission to use this?" she demanded.

Spencer ignored her. He ran over to his mother and gave her a big hug. As soon as Spencer let go, Mrs. Burton grabbed her car keys from his shirt.

As Spencer's dad reached to take his undershorts off of Spencer, the principal called out, "Wait, don't remove them yet. I need to get a picture for the newspaper."

Spencer reached down and picked up his little brother Jake. As he lifted The Terminator into the air, he heard someone yell, "Hey, what's the big idea? Somebody crashed my macaroni dinosaur and ate one of its legs."

Spencer looked at Jake and started to grin from one ear to the other. The Terminator smiled back, and when he did, a big piece of macaroni fell out of his mouth.

About the Author

Gary Hogg has always loved stories and has been creating them since he was a boy growing up in Idaho.

Gary is also a very popular storyteller. Each year he brings his humorous tales to life for thousands of people around the United States.

He lives in Huntsville, Utah, with his wife Sherry and their children, Jackson, Jonah, Annie, and Boone.

Here's a sneak peek
at the next

SPENCER'S *adventures*

#2 Garbage Snooper Surprise
by Gary Hogg

Grabbing the phone, Spencer blurted out, "Hey Josh, I just found out that we have a Garbage Snooper."

"You have a Garbage Snooper?" gasped Josh. "Wow! Unbelievable! Awesome! You lucky dog! Um, what's a Garbage Snooper?"

"It's kind of like a werewolf, but instead of ripping out your guts, it rips through your garbage."

"Does it eat your garbage?" asked Josh.

"I'm not sure," said Spencer. "But Snoopers are very dangerous and I'm going to catch this one all by myself."

"Let me help," begged Josh.

"No way," insisted Spencer. "This is serious business and you might get hurt."

"I have a box of chocolates that my grandma gave me," said Josh. "I'll share them with you."

"The candy your grandma gives you is always old and gross."

"These are good," said Josh. "They haven't even turned gray. My grandpa took a few sample bites out of some of them, but other than that, they're in great shape."

"Well," said Spencer, "chocolate is excellent brain food and two heads are better than one. All right, come on over."

Josh flew down the street on his bike. Soon he was at Spencer's door. The boys flopped down on the bed and began munching the brain food.

"Do you know where we can get a couple of grenades?" asked Spencer.

"No, but I know how to make a stink bomb."

"A good stink would be nice, but I think it will take more than that to stop this Snooper."

"How about a giant mousetrap?" asked Josh. "Do you think the Snooper likes cheese?"

"No, he just likes garbage. Hey, wait a minute, that's it!" exclaimed Spencer.

"What?" puzzled Josh.

Spencer sat up straight and started to talk fast. "The one thing we know for sure is that the Snooper loves garbage. So, let's give him some garbage that he'll never forget."

"What on earth are you talking about?"

"I'm talking about disguising myself as a pile of garbage. That way, when he starts snooping in our trash, I'll be right there to snag him."

"Oh, now I get it," said Josh. "It's brilliant! But where are we going to get a garbage disguise?"

"We'll make it," said Spencer. "Garbage day isn't until next Saturday. That gives us a whole week to collect trash for the garbage suit.

"Start hiding all of your family's garbage under your bed. On Friday, bring it over to my house and we'll use it to build the costume."

"Excellent," said Josh. "We'll give this Garbage Snooper the biggest surprise of his life."

TRIPLET TROUBLE

by Debbie Dadey and Marcia Thornton Jones

Triple your fun with these hilarious adventures!

Alex, Ashley, and Adam
mean well, but whenever they get involved
with something, it only means one thing —
trouble!

○ BBT90728-X	Triplet Trouble and the Cookie Contest	$2.99
○ BBT58107-4	Triplet Trouble and the Field Day Disaster	$2.99
○ BBT58106-6	Triplet Trouble and the Red Heart Race	$2.99
○ BBT25473-1	Triplet Trouble and the Runaway Reindeer	$2.99
○ BBT25472-3	Triplet Trouble and the Talent Show Mess	$2.99

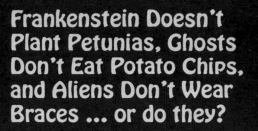

The Adventures of THE BAILEY SCHOOL KIDS™

Frankenstein Doesn't Plant Petunias, Ghosts Don't Eat Potato Chips, and Aliens Don't Wear Braces ... or do they?

Find out about the creepiest, weirdest, funniest things that happen to The Bailey School Kids!™ Collect and read them all!